NEW AMERICANS

Southeast Asian Americans

by Alan Wachtel

Series Consultant: Judith A. Warner, Ph.D.,
Professor of Sociology and Criminal Justice,
Texas A&M International University

Cavendish Square

Cavendish Square Publishing, LLC
2544 Clinton Street
Buffalo, NY 14224
www.cavendishsq.com

Library of Congress Cataloging-in-Publication Data

Wachtel, Alan.
New Americans: Southeast Asian Americans / by Alan Wachtel.
p. cm.
Includes bibliographical references and index.
ISBN 978-0-7614-4312-4
1. Immigrants—United States—History—Juvenile literature. 2. Southeast Asian Americans—History—Juvenile literature. 3. Ethnicity—United States—Juvenile literature. 4. Assimilation (Sociology)—United States—Juvenile literature. I. Title.
JV6455.W28 2010
305.895'073—dc22 2008055752

Developed for Cavendish Square Publishing by RJF Publishing LLC
Robert Famighetti, President
www.RJFpublishing.com
Design: Westgraphix LLC/Tammy West
Photo Research: Edward A. Thomas
Map Illustrator: Stefan Chabluk
Index: Nila Glikin

Photo credits: Cover, 1: © Jeff Greenberg/Alamy; 5, 24, 43, 62, 66, 69: AP/Wide World Photos; 6: © Catherine Karnow/CORBIS; 14: © Owen Franken/CORBIS; 16: Library of Congress LC-USZ62-68201; 19: Library of Congress LC-DIG-hec-06086; 21: New Mexico State University Library, Archives and Special Collections, Ms0431-5; 26: © Hulton-Deutsch Collection/CORBIS; 28: agefotostock; 34: © Michael Freeman/CORBIS; 36: Popperfoto/Getty Images; 38, 41, 44, 46, 50: Getty Images; 48: Time & Life Pictures/Getty Images; 53: © Jim West/Alamy; 56: © Richard Levine/Alamy; 59: Ben Twingley, Pensacola News Journal, Copyright 2008; 60: shutterstock; 63: Courtesy of the Filipino Reporter; 65: The Disney Channel/Photofest; 70: © David Butow/CORBIS SABA

Cover: Shoppers in the Little Saigon neighborhood of Westminster, California, which has a large Vietnamese-American community.

Printed in the United States of America

135642

CONTENTS

Introduction 4

CHAPTER ONE
The Southeast Asian-American Community Today 6

CHAPTER TWO
Earlier Generations 16

CHAPTER THREE
The New Immigrants 28

CHAPTER FOUR
Making a New Life 44

CHAPTER FIVE
Changing the American Culture 56

CHAPTER SIX
Looking to the Future 66

Facts About Filipino Americans 72

Facts About Vietnamese Americans 73

Glossary 74

To Find Out More 76

Bibliography 77

Index 78

Words defined in the glossary are in **bold** type the first time they appear in the text.

INTRODUCTION

The United States has embraced immigration for most of its history—and has been a destination of choice for people seeking a better life. Today hundreds of thousands of immigrants arrive each year to live and work and make their way in a new country. These "New Americans" come for many reasons, and they come from places all over the world. They bring with them new customs, languages, and traditions—and face many challenges in their adopted country. Over time, they and their children are changed by and become part of the American mainstream culture. At the same time, the mainstream is itself changed as it absorbs many elements of the immigrants' cultures, from ethnic foods to ideas from non-Western belief systems. An understanding of the New Americans, and how they will form part of the American future, is essential for everyone.

This series focuses on recent immigrants from eight major countries and regions: the Caribbean and Central America, China, India and other South Asian countries, Korea, Mexico, Russia and Eastern Europe, Southeast Asia, and West Africa.

Each of these geographic areas is a major source of the millions of immigrants who have come to the United States in the last decades of the twentieth century and the beginning of the twenty-first. For many of these people, the opportunity to move to the United States was opened up by the major

New Americans being sworn in as U.S. citizens.

changes in U.S. immigration law that occurred in the 1960s. For others, the opportunity or imperative to immigrate was triggered by events in their own countries, such as the collapse of Communism in Eastern Europe or civil wars in Central America.

Some of the New Americans found sizable communities of Americans from the same ethnic background and had the benefit of "ethnic neighborhoods" to move into where they could feel welcome and get help adjusting to American life. Many of these communities originated in a previous major wave of immigration, from the 1880s to 1920. Some of the New Americans found very few predecessors to ease the transition as they faced the challenges of adjustment.

These volumes tell the stories of the New Americans, including the personal accounts of a number of immigrants and their children who agreed to be interviewed by some of the authors. As you read, you will learn about the countries of origin and the cultures of these newcomers to American society. You will learn, as well, about how the New Americans are enriching, as they adapt to, American life.

Judith A. Warner, Ph.D.
Professor of Sociology and Criminal Justice
Texas A&M International University

The Little Saigon neighborhood in Westminster, in southern California, is the heart of one of the largest Vietnamese-American communities in the United States.

CHAPTER ONE

THE SOUTHEAST ASIAN-AMERICAN COMMUNITY TODAY

Take a walk down Bolsa Avenue, in Westminster, California, and you will be in the heart of Little Saigon. Westminster is located in Orange County. This area has one of the largest Vietnamese-American communities in the United States. Little Saigon is named after the former capital of South Vietnam. In Little Saigon, the streets are full of people speaking Vietnamese. Stores have signs in Vietnamese that say what the store sells and who owns it. Shoppers buy fresh vegetables, rice, and Vietnamese newspapers and magazines. Restaurants, cafés, and markets in Little Saigon feature Vietnamese food, from bowls of *pho* soup to tasty *banh mi* sandwiches. Vietnamese Americans of all ages live in or visit Little Saigon to be among others who share their culture and traditions. Other Americans also head to Little Saigon to experience Vietnamese-American culture.

States with the Most Vietnamese Americans

California	447,032
Texas	134,961
Washington	46,149
Virginia	37,309
Massachusetts	33,962
Florida	33,190
Pennsylvania	30,037
Georgia	29,016
Louisiana	24,358
New York	23,818

Source: U.S. Bureau of the Census, 2000 Census data
Note: Census Bureau 2006 population estimates do not give breadowns by state for states with fewer than 65,000 Vietnamese Americans.

Southeast Asian Americans live all over the United States, but the state with the largest number is California. In 2006, California had about 1.1 million Filipino Americans, 534,000 Vietnamese Americans, 87,000 Cambodian Americans, 71,000 Hmong Americans, and 66,000 Laotian Americans. California's Filipino-American population is the largest of any U.S. state. California also has the largest number of Vietnamese Americans, although many also live in Texas (184,000 in 2006) and Washington (68,000). Many states have smaller concentrations of Southeast Asian Americans. Minnesota and Wisconsin, for example, have many Hmong Americans.

Countries of Origin

Filipino Americans have their roots in the Philippines. The Philippines is a country made up of an archipelago (that is, a group of islands) that lies east of mainland Asia, between the South China Sea and the Philippine Sea. For almost fifty years, the Philippines was a colony of the United States. Filipino Americans make up the largest group of Southeast Asian Americans. In 2006, according to U.S. Census Bureau estimates, more than 2.3 million Filipino Americans were living in the United States.

Most other Southeast Asian Americans have their roots in three countries in Indochina—Vietnam, Cambodia, and Laos. Indochina is the peninsula in Southeast Asia that lies south of China and east of India. Vietnam stretches along the eastern side of the **peninsula**. To its west are Laos and Cambodia. From the mid-1960s to 1973, the United States

Southeast Asian Nations

Although sometimes the name Indochina is used to refer only to Vietnam, Cambodia, and Laos, other countries often considered part of Indochina include Myanmar (the official name for the country formerly called Burma), Thailand, Malaysia, and Singapore. Besides the Philippines and the countries of Indochina, Southeast Asia also includes the large island nation of Indonesia and the small countries of East Timor and Brunei. Aside from the Philippines, Vietnam, Cambodia, and Laos, the other countries of Southeast Asia have not been sources of large-scale immigration to the United States, and the number of Americans with origins in these countries is fairly small. For example, in 2006, Thai Americans numbered about 150,000 and Indonesian Americans about 66,000; Malaysian Americans numbered 10,690, according to the 2000 U.S. Census.

fought in the Vietnam War in order to try to stop the spread of **Communism**. Although most of the fighting took place in Vietnam, the war spilled over into Cambodia and Laos as well. Laotian Americans and Hmong Americans both come from Laos. The Hmong are an **ethnic** group from the highlands of Laos. During the Vietnam War, the Hmong sided with the United States. In 2006, there were nearly 1.5 million Vietnamese Americans, more than 200,000 Cambodian Americans, more than

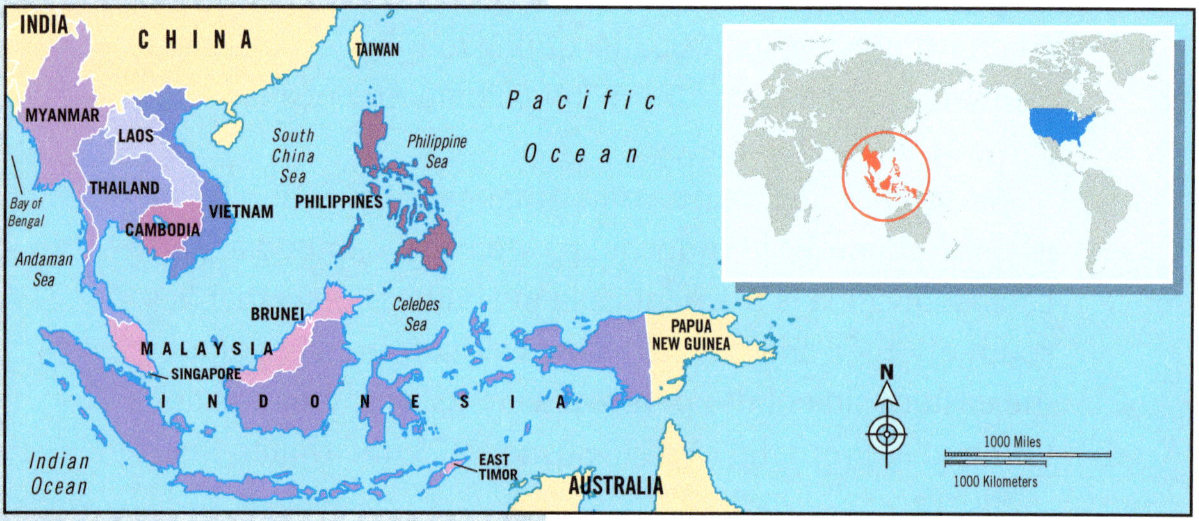

Southeast Asian Americans	
Origin	**Number of People**
Filipino Americans	2,328,097
Vietnamese Americans	1,475,798
Cambodian Americans	212,157
Hmong Americans	205,101
Laotian Americans	194,320
Thai Americans	150,414

Source: U.S. Bureau of the Census, 2006 estimates

200,000 Hmong Americans, and almost 200,000 Laotian Americans living in the United States.

Successes and Struggles

In many ways, Filipino Americans are **assimilated** into the American population. Of all Southeast Asian-American groups, they have the longest history in the United States. According to the U.S. Census Bureau's 2006 American Community Survey, about 78 percent of Filipino Americans speak English very well. They tend to be successful in the American workforce. More than 40 percent of working Filipino Americans hold high-status **managerial** and

States with the Most Filipino Americans

California	1,100,767
Hawaii	182,767
Illinois	114,266
New York	107,418
New Jersey	105,806
Texas	95,436
Washington	80,896
Florida	74,826
Nevada	73,261

Source: U.S. Bureau of the Census, 2006 estimates

professional jobs. The average **per capita** income of Filipino Americans is over $27,000 a year—almost $2,000 more than the average for all Americans.

In contrast, Vietnamese Americans and other Southeast Asian-American groups face many struggles. Very few members of these ethnic groups lived in the United States before the Vietnam War. When the war ended, hundreds of thousands of Vietnamese, Cambodians, ethnic Laotians, and Hmong came to the United States as **refugees**. Today, large numbers of them still struggle with English, hold low-status jobs, and remain poor. According to the 2006 American Community Survey, almost 53 percent of Vietnamese Americans speak English "less than very well." The other groups from Indochina have, on average, only slightly better English skills. Economically, Vietnamese Americans are the best off of the groups from Indochina. Their yearly per capita income, however, was just $21,447 in 2006. The other Indochinese groups faced even greater economic challenges. Per capita income for Laotian Americans was $16,175 a year, and per capita income for Cambodian Americans was $15,138—which is well below the national average of $25,267. Per capita income for Hmong Americans was $9,750.

One reason for the low incomes of Cambodian Americans, Laotian Americans, and Hmong Americans may be age. All three of these groups have a **median** age much lower than the national median age. (The median is a midpoint number that divides a group in half; whatever a group's median age is, half the people in that group will

Hmong-American Enclaves in Wisconsin and Minnesota

Like many other Southeast Asian-American groups, many Hmong Americans live together in ethnic neighborhoods, which are sometimes also called ethnic **enclaves**. Some of their enclaves, however, are far from the largest U.S. cities. Although many Hmong Americans live in California, large numbers also live in the Upper Midwest, especially in Minnesota and Wisconsin. Many Hmong Americans have moved to this region from California because of job opportunities and a significantly lower cost of living. The city of Milwaukee has the largest number of Hmong Americans in Wisconsin. But there are also sizable Hmong-American communities in the cities of Wausau and Sheboygan, and in 2007, a new Hmong cultural center opened in La Crosse, Wisconsin. In Minnesota, the Minneapolis-Saint Paul area has a large Hmong-American population. Both Wisconsin and Minnesota have Hmong-American radio stations, many Hmong American-owned businesses, and Hmong-American cultural organizations. These areas also have Hmong restaurants. Traditional Hmong food is usually simple and made with fresh ingredients. One reason for this is that, in Laos, many Hmong did not have refrigerators and ovens. Soups that include boiled chicken, beef, or pork, fresh vegetables, and herbs are popular. Vegetables and herbs used in Hmong cooking include Thai eggplant, bitter melon, fresh garlic, green onions (scallions), lemongrass, and cilantro. Fresh tropical fruits and rice are also important in Hmong cuisine. Many Hmong restaurants do not strongly advertise traditional Hmong food. They may serve both Hmong dishes and another, better-known Southeast Asian cuisine, such as Thai food.

Customers shop for fresh produce at a farmers' market in Minnesota run mostly by Hmong Americans.

be older and half will be younger.) The median age for all Americans in 2006 was about thirty-six years old. The median age for Laotian Americans was about thirty, while the median age for Cambodian Americans was about twenty-eight. Hmong Americans were the youngest group, with a median age of only about nineteen. Therefore, all three of these groups, and especially the Hmong, include a relatively large number of people too young to be working.

Bringing Southeast Asia to the United States

Southeast Asian Americans have brought the flavors of their countries of origin to the United States. Like other American **immigrant** groups, many of them live together in ethnic neighborhoods. The Filipino-American neighborhood in Los Angeles is called Historic Filipinotown. It features a huge mural depicting Filipino history, a Filipino library, Filipino restaurants, churches that cater to Filipino Americans, and a memorial to Filipino Americans who lost their lives in World War II.

A number of Vietnamese neighborhoods around the United States are called Little Saigons, such as the one in Westminster, California. Houston, Texas, has a Little Saigon area that features Vietnamese shops and restaurants. Los Angeles, which has the largest Thai population outside of Thailand, has a neighborhood called Thai Town. It includes Thai restaurants, bookstores, and silk shops. The city government of Los Angeles officially recognized Thai Town in 1999. In addition, Long Beach, California, has an area called Cambodia Town.

These illustrations of the Manilamen's way of life in Louisiana were published in a magazine in 1883.

CHAPTER TWO

EARLIER GENERATIONS

The Philippines has a long history of contact with the United States. Spain took control of the Philippines and made it a colony in 1565. Filipinos began taking part in the Spanish **galleon** trade (trade that took place on Spanish ships between the Philippines and Mexico, which was then also a Spanish colony). The first Filipinos came to what is now the United States in 1763—even before the American Revolution. Near New Orleans, Louisiana, they escaped from Spanish ships, on which they were not treated well. They set up a fishing village called Saint Malo in the marshland near New Orleans.

The Manilamen

These first Filipino Americans became known as the Manilamen. The name comes from Manila, the capital city of the Philippines. Over time, more escaped Filipino sailors joined them. Manilamen also sent money to friends in the Philippines. Some of these friends came to live in the Saint Malo settlement, too.

Very few people knew about the Manilamen until 1883. That year, a newspaper from New Orleans organized a boat trip to Saint Malo. Journalist Lafcadio Hearn wrote articles describing the lives of the Manilamen. In addition, an artist came along to draw pictures of the Manilamen and their homes.

The lives of the Manilamen were simple. They lived in wooden houses that stood on wooden supports in the marshes. Their diet consisted mainly of raw fish combined with oil and vinegar, and they had few luxuries. In spite of being in Louisiana, the Manilamen lived mainly by their own rules. They did not have police officers or a tax system. The oldest man in the village settled disputes. Only a few non-Filipino men lived among the Manilamen. The Manilamen married local women, including Cajuns (descendants of French settlers who had immigrated to Louisiana from Acadia in eastern Canada) and American Indians. Most of their wives and children lived around New Orleans, while the men stayed in the fishing village.

An American Colony

The end of the nineteenth century brought major changes to the Philippines. In 1898, the United States fought against Spain in the Spanish-American War. Commodore George Dewey of the U.S. Navy had orders to fight Spain in the

Members of the U.S. Signal Corps at work in the Philippines in 1916. The Corps put up telephone and telegraph lines during the period of American colonial rule.

Philippines if war broke out. As soon as war was declared in late April, he sailed his ships for the Philippines. On May 1, 1898, Dewey's ships arrived in Manila Bay, and they soon defeated Spain's naval forces in the Philippines in a quick battle. The Spanish-American War ended with the signing of the Treaty of Paris on December 10, 1898. In that treaty, Spain gave control of the Philippines to the United States. This made the Philippines an American colony, angering many Filipinos, who had hoped the end of Spanish rule would result in independence for the Philippines. At the same time, the change of control brought the Philippines and the United States closer together.

Filipinos became U.S. **nationals**. The United States put an American-style educational system in place in the colony. Schools taught lessons in English, and students learned about American history and government. The United States also helped to develop the **infrastructure** of the Philippines. At the end of Spanish rule, the country had fewer than 1,000 miles (1,600 kilometers) of roads. About thirty-five years later, the Philippines had closer to 13,000 mi. (20,900 km) of roads. The United States also helped build the country's railway system. This infrastructure supported growth in the economy of the Philippines. Sugar, textiles, cigarettes, coconut oil, lumber, and gold mining all became growing industries.

Most importantly, the United States brought American-style government to the Philippines. American rule was harsh at first, and the top official in the Philippines always was an American governor-general. But Filipinos came to know many important features of American government. Freedom of speech, freedom of religion, and freedom of the press all became part of Filipino life. Filipinos learned about and took part in their own government. At first, the colonial government included far more Americans than Filipinos. By the early 1920s, it included 13,240 Filipinos and only 614 Americans. Eventually, Filipinos elected members of their own Senate and House of Representatives. The country's judicial system also came to include many Filipino judges. Since Filipinos got to know American culture so well under colonial rule, those who immigrated to the United States were well prepared for American life.

Pensionados

Another way Filipinos got to know American life was by studying in the United States. In the early 1900s, some Filipinos came to the United States to attend college. In 1903, the U.S. Congress passed the Pensionado Act. This law created a program that sent young Filipinos to American universities. They were called *pensionados*. Most of the pensionados were from wealthy families that had connections to the colonial government. Pensionados attended universities such as Harvard, Stanford, Cornell, Purdue, the University of California at Berkeley, and the University of Illinois. The government of the Philippines paid for their schooling. In all,

A group of pensionados visiting the St. Louis world's fair in the early 1900s.

about five hundred pensionados studied in the United States. When they went back to the Philippines, many of them became leaders in government and business. The pensionado program ended in 1910.

Filipino Immigrants

As U.S. nationals, Filipinos could move from the Philippines to the United States. In the early 1900s, the U.S. government generally prohibited or severely restricted immigration from such Asian countries as China, Japan, and Korea. But Filipinos did not face these restrictions. After the pensionado program ended, thousands of other Filipino students came to the United States. Without scholarship support, they had a much harder time making ends meet and finishing school. Many of these students worked in unskilled jobs in hotels and restaurants.

Other Filipinos came to the United States just to work. In 1907, about two hundred Filipino laborers arrived in the U.S. territory of Hawaii. The states of California and Washington, on the Pacific coast, were among the first on the mainland United States to have sizable Filipino populations. By the late 1920s and early 1930s, Filipinos had also settled in the Midwest, in such states as Illinois, Michigan, and Minnesota. In all of these states, Filipinos started newspapers, community groups, and professional groups. These included the *Filipino Forum*, a newspaper for Filipinos in the Pacific Northwest, and the Filipino Nurses' Association of Chicago. One small part of Filipino culture that had become a craze in the United States by the 1930s was the yo-yo. Pedro Flores—the father of the American yo-yo—was a Filipino American.

Filipinos started working for the U.S. Navy almost as soon as the United States took over the Philippines. They worked mostly as stewards and mess boys. By 1903, nine Filipinos were members of the Navy. The number quickly increased. By the time the United States fought in World War I in 1917–1918, the Navy included about 6,000 Filipinos. That number grew to 25,000 by 1930.

In the mid–1930s, U.S. President Franklin D. Roosevelt signed the Philippine Independence Act, intended to prepare the Philippines for independence on July 4, 1946. But this law, sometimes known as the Tydings-McDuffie Act, also changed the status of Filipinos from nationals to **aliens**, and it put strict limits on Filipino immigration.

Before 1946, however, the United States needed the help of Filipinos in World War II. The United States entered the war when Japanese planes attacked Pearl Harbor, the large U.S. Navy base in Hawaii, on December 7, 1941. Three days later, on December 10, 1941, Japan invaded the Philippines. To help in the fight against Japan, the United States recruited Filipinos to join its armed forces. Many Filipino soldiers fought in the First and Second Filipino Infantry Regiments. After the war, many of these Filipino soldiers became U.S. citizens. In the 1940s, there were about forty unmarried Filipino-American men for every unmarried Filipino-American woman. When the United States sent troops to fight in the Philippines, many Filipino-American soldiers returned with Filipino brides.

A U.S. Marine Corps sergeant trains Filipinos fighting with American troops in the Philippines in 1942, during World War II.

Around the same time, the laws of the United States changed in favor of Filipinos. In May 1945, the U.S. Supreme Court ruled that Filipinos had to be considered nationals, not aliens. About a year later, on June 14, 1946, U.S. President Harry Truman signed the Filipino Naturalization Bill, which made Filipino immigrants eligible to become U.S. citizens (before that citizenship eligibility was severely restricted). Soon after, another new law gave automatic citizenship to Filipinos living in the United States who had arrived before March 24, 1934. The 1960 U.S. Census counted 201,746 Filipino Americans.

Troubles in a New Country

Although many Filipinos who came to the United States during the time the Philippines was a U.S. colony quickly established themselves, their new country did not always welcome them. Filipinos faced discrimination in hiring for jobs, housing, education, and almost all parts of American life. Some Americans were afraid that Filipino immigrants would take their jobs. Sometimes Filipinos faced threats and violence from Americans. In 1928, a mob of white workers tried to chase a group of Filipino workers out of the town of Wenatchee, Washington. Filipinos also faced petty acts of discrimination. For example, in 1928, at the University of Washington, Filipino students were barred from using a YMCA school social room. Filipino Americans were sometimes refused service in restaurants and hotels. Some businesses posted signs saying "Absolutely no Filipinos allowed." Filipinos in California who wanted to

Chang and Eng Bunker

Among the earliest Southeast Asians to come to the United States were Chang and Eng. Chang and Eng were famous **conjoined** twins. They were born in Siam (which later became Thailand) in 1811. The twins were joined at the chest. At first, many people who saw Chang and Eng were scared of them. Some people thought they would bring bad luck, and the king of Siam even wanted to have them killed. In spite of this, they grew and learned how to deal with being joined together. To the amazement of many, they could run, jump, and swim. Chang and Eng were working to support their family when they were discovered by Robert Hunter, a British merchant. Hunter thought he could make money for himself and Chang and Eng. Hunter and Captain Abel Coffin, an American painter, managed the brothers' career. They toured Chang and Eng around the world as the stars of a show that exhibited their unusual life and abilities. Most of the time, the businessmen treated Chang and Eng well.

Chang and Eng began running their own career in 1832. Eventually, they made enough money to buy a farm in North Carolina. Chang and Eng became U.S. citizens and took the last name "Bunker." Soon after, the brothers married two sisters. Chang married Adelaide Yates. Eng married her sister, Sally. Both couples had many children. The twin brothers and their wives did not always get along, but they managed to live together for several years. Eventually two separate homes were set up, with Chang and Eng spending some time in each of the two. Money problems forced Chang and Eng to return to show business in 1860, and the Civil War (1861–1865) ruined their farming business. They died on the same day in 1874, with Chang passing away first.

A short story called "The Siamese Twins" by the nineteenth-century American writer Mark Twain and a novel called *Chang and Eng* published in 2000 were based on the lives of Chang and Eng Bunker.

The conjoined twins Chang and Eng Bunker are shown here in a photo taken around 1870.

marry whites could not because of a law against interracial marriage. This law was not overturned until 1948.

Other Southeast Asian Immigrants

The early Filipino immigrants laid the foundation for Filipino Americans to become the largest and most successful Southeast Asian-American group in the United States. They were the only Southeast Asian Americans who came to the United States in large numbers before the 1970s. The numbers of Vietnamese, Laotian, and Cambodian immigrants before the 1970s were extremely small. From 1952 to 1959, 219 Vietnamese, 6 Cambodians, and 1 Laotian arrived in the United States, according to U.S. immigration records. During the 1960s—as conflict in the region grew—3,167 Vietnamese, 98 Cambodians, and 69 Laotians arrived. These Vietnamese, Cambodians, and Laotians included college students from elite families, some of whom chose to stay in the United States permanently, and the spouses of American military personnel. With the United States getting more involved in the Vietnam War, the number of Vietnamese immigrants shot up in the early 1970s. From 1970 to 1975, 14,661 Vietnamese immigrants came to the United States. During the same time, 286 Cambodians and 292 Laotians immigrated.

In addition to early Vietnamese, Cambodian, and Laotian immigrants, small numbers of immigrants came from other Southeast Asian countries. For example, some Burmese arrived in the early 1960s, fleeing harsh military rule in their native country.

A Filipino-American nurse assists a patient at a California nursing home.

CHAPTER THREE

THE NEW IMMIGRANTS

During the years after World War II and through the early 1960s, Filipinos continued coming to the United States. Filipino-American communities continued to grow. In 1962, Filipino immigration got a boost from the U.S. government, which began to allow foreign medical professionals to apply for **permanent resident visas**. Some doctors in the Philippines took the opportunity to come to the United States, and many Filipinos studying at American medical schools took the opportunity to stay.

A New Immigration Policy

Then, in 1965, the Immigration and Nationality Act opened the doors of the United States to even more Filipinos. This law ended specific quotas on the number of immigrants permitted from each country (a quota system, in effect for more than forty years, that had favored immigrants from Northern and Western Europe). Instead, it set an overall limit on immigrants from the Eastern Hemisphere (the part of the world that includes Asia, Europe, and Africa) and, within that limit, allowed up to 20,000 immigrants per year from a single country. Another part of the new law allowed immediate family members (spouses, children, and parents) of immigrants who were already U.S. citizens to enter the country without being counted against the 20,000 maximum. As a result, Filipino immigration grew. Filipinos had many reasons for coming to the United States, including better job and educational opportunities. Many Filipinos also wanted to escape the dictatorial rule of Ferdinand Marcos, who had become president of the Philippines in 1965. In 1970, more than 30,000 Filipino immigrants arrived. From 1970 to 1980, the Filipino-American population more than doubled. It rose from 343,060 to 774,652. Over the next ten years it almost doubled again,

Filipino Americans	
1970	343,060
1980	774,652
1990	1,460,770
2000	1,850,314
2006	2,328,097

Source: U.S. Bureau of the Census

rising to 1,460,770 in 1990. In the early 1990s, more than 60,000 Filipino immigrants were arriving each year. The 2000 U.S. Census counted 1,850,314 Filipino Americans, and the Filipino-American population had increased by almost another half-million by 2006.

Vietnam: A Complicated War

After the end of World War II, the cold war began. The cold war was a conflict between **Communist** and non-Communist countries. The most powerful Communist country was the Soviet Union. The most powerful non-Communist country was the United States. During the cold war, the armies of the United States and the Soviet Union did not directly fight each other. Instead, the two countries competed for influence in other countries around the world. The United States was eager to prevent the spread of Communism. To do this, it supported anti-Communist groups and governments in countries where there was a threat that Communists might take over. During the cold war, Vietnam and its neighboring countries in Indochina became the bloodiest front of the war against Communism.

In the mid–1800s, Vietnam became a French colony. It was occupied by Japan in World War II. After Japan's defeat and the end of the war in 1945, France tried to reclaim its colony, but a Communist-led group called the Viet Minh declared Vietnam's independence. French troops fought for almost a decade against the Viet Minh, which had more support in northern Vietnam than in the south. After the

French forces suffered a major defeat in 1954, an agreement was reached dividing Vietnam in two. North Vietnam became a Communist country, headed by Ho Chi Minh (who was the leader of the Viet Minh). South Vietnam had a non-Communist government.

The U.S. government was concerned that North Vietnam supported Communists in the South and was trying to take over the South. In an effort to prevent this, beginning in the 1950s, the United States sent military advisers to South Vietnam to help its government fight Communists there. As the war dragged on, beginning in 1965, the United States sent hundreds of thousands of troops to South Vietnam, where they fought both South Vietnamese Communists (known as the Viet Cong) and North Vietnamese troops that invaded the South.

The War Spreads

During the war, Communist forces in South Vietnam received supplies from the North transported down a network of jungle paths that became known as the Ho Chi Minh trail. Much of the trail ran through Laos, which also had its own civil war between Communist and non-Communist groups. Besides heavily bombing the Ho Chi Minh trail with warplanes, the United States recruited Laotians, and particularly members of the Hmong ethnic group, to fight the Laotian Communists and to try to cut off supplies moving down the Ho Chi Minh trail. By 1970, the war had also spread to Cambodia. Communist forces were using areas in eastern Cambodia to prepare for attacks into

Vietnam and to retreat safely when pursued by American or South Vietnamese troops. When American forces invaded Cambodia to attack these areas, North Vietnam supported a Communist overthrow of the Cambodian government. By 1975, the Communist Khmer Rouge, led by dictator Pol Pot, controlled Cambodia. A Communist government also gained control in Laos in 1975.

In Vietnam itself, bloody and destructive fighting went on for years, with no clear-cut result. The war became increasingly unpopular in the United States. In 1973, as part of an agreement negotiated with North Vietnam, the United States withdrew all of its troops from South Vietnam. Two years later, in 1975, North Vietnamese and Viet Cong forces attacked and captured the South Vietnamese capital of Saigon. The South Vietnamese government surrendered. Vietnam became a unified Communist country (and Saigon was renamed Ho Chi Minh City).

The result of this complicated war was a huge refugee crisis. Vietnamese people who had supported, worked for, and fought on the side of the United States were in great danger after the Communist takeover of the South. This was also true in Laos, especially for the Hmong. Meanwhile, the Khmer Rouge government was soaking Cambodia in blood. It tried to kill all opponents and people it thought could be opponents, including people with formal education. (The Khmer Rouge even targeted people who wore eyeglasses, on the assumption that such people were educated and posed a threat.) It forced people to leave the cities and move to rural labor camps. Between 1975

The Killing Fields

In 1984, a movie came out that showed the horrors of Khmer Rouge rule in Cambodia. The movie involved two of the most famous Cambodian Americans, Dith Pran and Dr. Haing S. Ngor.

Called *The Killing Fields*, the movie tells the true story of Sydney Schanberg, an American, and Dith Pran, a Cambodian. Schanberg and Dith Pran were journalists for the *New York Times*. Their job was to report about Cambodia. When the Khmer Rouge took over, Schanberg was able to leave, but Dith Pran was captured. The movie then shows Dith Pran's struggle to survive the brutal Khmer Rouge labor camps, his dangerous escape from Cambodia, and his arrival in the United States. Dith Pran worked for the *New York Times* until his death in 2008.

In *The Killing Fields*, Dith Pran was played by Dr. Haing S. Ngor. Ngor had first-hand experience surviving the brutality of the Khmer Rouge. Before he was an actor, Ngor was a doctor in Cambodia. Knowing that the Khmer Rouge wanted to kill all educated people, Ngor pretended he was not a doctor. When the Khmer Rouge fell, he came to the United States as a refugee. Playing Dith Pran was Ngor's first acting role. For his performance, Ngor won an Academy Award for Best Supporting Actor. He continued acting, although *The Killing Fields* remained his most famous movie. Ngor also became a human rights activist who worked to help Cambodian refugees. He was murdered by robbers in 1996.

The Killing Fields is not the only American movie to focus on the life of a Southeast Asian American. Director Oliver Stone's 1993 film *Heaven and Earth* was based on a memoir written by Le Ly Hayslip, a Vietnamese girl who flees her village with her mother during the Vietnam War, struggles to survive in Saigon, and eventually marries an American officer and comes to the United States.

Dith Pran (*left*) and Haing S. Ngor during a return visit to Cambodia in more peaceful times.

and 1979 (when the Khmer Rouge government was overthrown), at least 1.5 million Cambodians were killed by the Khmer Rouge or died of such causes as starvation and disease as a result of Khmer Rouge policies. Many Cambodians who could escape fled the country.

Waves of Vietnamese Refugees

The United States knew it had played a major role in the war in Southeast Asia. The U.S. government did not want to turn its back on people who had helped it in the war. At the end of April 1975—just before Saigon fell to the Communists—the U.S. government began bringing refugees to the United States. The 1975 Indochina Migration and Refugee Assistance Act provided the legal basis for their entry.

The refugees did not come all at once. Experts speak of waves of refugees, or large migrations. The first wave of refugees from Vietnam numbered more than 125,000 people. Most of them were taken out of Vietnam in 1975 in helicopters, airplanes, and boats from the United States and other countries. Their departure was not well planned. The United States did not foresee how many Vietnamese it would need to get out of Vietnam. Many Vietnamese who left their country at this time say that—with Communist forces closing in—they heard bombs, gunfire, and screaming as they were leaving. One Vietnamese woman remembers:

> "[A]ll of these people were trying to get on the plane at the airport. . . . I saw people jamming the door. . . . The shelling came closer, and the plane took off with people still hanging at the door."

Desperate to leave, some Vietnamese people try to board one of the last U.S. planes out of Saigon before the city fell to North Vietnamese and Viet Cong Communist forces in April 1975.

Many people in the first wave of Vietnamese refugees were members of the South Vietnamese army or had worked with the United States in other ways. Their family members were also trying to leave. A number of these people were well educated and knew some English. About half of them were Christian, which made them a minority group in Vietnam. If they had stayed in Vietnam after the Communists took over, they could have been in great danger. They were first taken to refugee camps in countries including the Philippines, Thailand, and Malaysia. Then, they were sent to the United States. Once in the United States, they were resettled all over the country. The U.S. government funded fourteen **voluntary agencies** that helped the refugees begin their new lives. The reason the refugees were spread around the country was so that no single community would have to bear the burden of a large group coming in all at once and needing social services. Over time, however, many of the Vietnamese refugees moved to areas where they could live around others from their native country.

The second wave of Vietnamese refugees began about two years after the first wave. The refugees of the second wave were fleeing the difficult conditions in Vietnam and the harsh rule of the Communist government that took over the South. Although the war was over, life in Vietnam was still extremely hard. In part, this was because so many years of warfare had seriously damaged the country's economy. The Communist government forced many people in the South out of cities to work on

One Person's Story: Le Tan Si

Le Tan Si came from a family of seven. He was the first member of his family to leave Vietnam. In an interview for the book *The Far East Comes Near: Autobiographical Accounts of Southeast Asian Students in America*, Le Tan Si describes the hardships of escaping Vietnam as a boat person. He was in his late teens at the time:

> "Around 9:00 P.M. on June 4, 1979, . . . our boat departed in good weather with fifty-eight people on board. Our boat operated safely for the next two days. . . . Around 2:00 A.M. on June 6, 1979, the overworked engine broke down. . . . During this period, I left my life to chance. . . . We were frightened because we had no control over a boat with a dead engine. Meanwhile, we anchored to make the boat safer. I thought about my life, my parents, and friends, and I also wondered if my death was near. Our supply of food and water were gradually decreasing as our boat drifted on the sea, so we starved."

Le Tan Si also describes surviving brutal pirate attacks before his boat was rescued by fishermen. He finally made it to a refugee camp in Indonesia. In August 1980, he arrived in the United States. The next year, Le Tan Si reunited with his brother in Boston, Massachusetts.

In the late 1970s, hundreds of thousands of Vietnamese "boat people" fled their country in small craft that were often not very seaworthy.

farms. Many Communist soldiers stole from people whatever valuables they could. Poverty gripped the country. In the late 1970s, many Vietnamese decided to risk their lives to leave. Most of these desperate people tried to leave by boat. Many of the boats they used were in poor condition. Still, people crowded into them. As the packed boats left Vietnam, they sometimes faced deadly storms. Worse were the pirate attacks. Not only did the pirates steal whatever they could, but they also murdered and raped.

The refugees who escaped Vietnam by boat became known as "boat people." Between 1977 and 1979, about 300,000 boat people fled Vietnam. Many of the boat people who were lucky enough to make it to land ended up in refugee camps in Thailand. Life in these camps was also horrible. The camps were dirty, and there was often not enough food. From the camps, the boat people were resettled in various countries, including Australia, Canada, France, and the United States. The largest number went to the United States.

Later, several programs and laws helped Vietnamese refugees who wanted to come to the United States. In 1979, the Orderly Departure Program was begun. This program was created by the United Nations and the government of Vietnam. Around the same time, the United States passed the Refugee Act of 1980. Under this new law, as well as the 1965 Immigration and Nationality Act, the United States took in refugees leaving Vietnam as part of the Orderly Departure Program. These refugees included those who had family members already in the United States and more

One Person's Story: Dao Vang

Dao Vang is a Hmong American who came to the United States from Laos with his family in 1976, when he was thirteen years old. He talks about his first experiences in his new country:

> "We arrived in La Crosse from Chicago. It was about 10 P.M. In the dark, all we could see were the lights and the cars on the road. Our sponsors [an American family that had volunteered to help the refugee family get settled] took us to Sparta, Wisconsin. The next day we saw how different everything was. Sparta was a small town with about six thousand people. In Sparta, it was shocking how different the people and food were. We eat rice, and our sponsors there did not know where to get rice for us. It was not until one month later before our sponsors took us to La Crosse, where we could buy rice. Another big difference is that, in Laos, we lived in a small village. There was no electricity and no running water, and because of this, I think our adjustment was very different from the refugees who came from major cities in their country."

people who had worked with the United States in the past. In addition, the **Amerasian** Homecoming Act of 1987 opened the country to the children of Vietnamese mothers and American fathers (who most often were U.S. soldiers who had served in Vietnam). Amerasians suffered severe discrimination in Vietnam. The United States accepted Amerasians born between 1962 and 1976. They did not have to give proof that their father was American. All that was required was for them to look like they had one Asian parent and one white or black parent.

The 125,000 Vietnamese refugees who came to the United States in 1975 is by far the largest number for any single year. In 1980, 95,200 Vietnamese refugees arrived. The next year, 65,279 came. For the rest of the 1980s, about 26,000 arrived each year. About 200,000 arrived in the 1990s. In 1992, some of the Vietnamese refugees who came to the United States were Montagnards. The

A Hmong refugee and her mother shed tears of joy as they are reunited in Fresno, California.

Montagnards are a Vietnamese ethnic group that sided with the United States in the Vietnam War. Although the United States pulled out of Vietnam in the 1970s, the Montagnards kept fighting the Communists until 1992. Over time, the tide of Vietnamese refugees has slowed. In 2000, 3,817 refugees arrived from Vietnam. Since then, the number has averaged about 2,200 a year.

Flight from Laos and Cambodia

In addition to the waves of Vietnamese refugees, there were also waves of refugees from Laos and Cambodia. Like the Vietnamese, refugees started coming from both countries in 1975. That year, about 800 refugees came from Laos and about 4,600 came from Cambodia. The refugees from Laos included both ethnic Lao and Hmong. More than 100,000 refugees from Laos came to the United States from 1975 to 1980. About 30,000 of these people were Hmong. Thousands more refugees came from Laos each year through the early 1990s. Their numbers dropped off from 2000 to 2003. Between 2004 and 2006, however, the United States took in more than 15,000 Hmong refugees. These people had been living for many years in refugee camps in Thailand. About 75 percent of them went to California, Minnesota, and Wisconsin.

The largest influx of Cambodian refugees came after the Khmer Rouge government fell in 1979. Between 1980 and 1985, more than 100,000 Cambodian refugees came to the United States. By the early 1990s, only about a hundred were arriving each year, and that number dropped further in the early twenty-first century.

Other Immigrants

After 1975, a number of people from Thailand began coming to the United States. During the 1970s, about 44,000 arrived. In the 1980s, the number of Thai immigrants was about 64,000.

After the military took control of the government of Burma in 1988 (the next year it changed the country's name to Myanmar), more Burmese people began coming to the United States. As the military government continued to treat political opponents harshly and resisted efforts to return to democracy, in the early years of the twenty-first

A Burmese family in their apartment near Seattle in 2008, a year after arriving in the United States from a refugee camp in Thailand.

century, more than 12,000 Burmese entered the United States. In 2007, Burmese were more numerous than any other refugee group. That year, almost 14,000 Burmese refugees arrived in the United States, fleeing both political persecution and persecution of members of certain ethnic groups. Refugees continued arriving in 2008. Many of them have settled in New York and other large cities, where they must adjust to a way of life very different from what they have known in their native country. For some of the children, life in the United States may be their first experience living outside a refugee camp.

A Hmong immigrant (*right*) in California takes part in a class on job-interviewing tips, including the importance of a firm handshake.

CHAPTER FOUR

MAKING A NEW LIFE

Many new immigrants need some help in getting used to life in the United States. Filipino immigrants can often get help from family members already in the country or from others in the Filipino-American community. Most refugees from Indochina entering the country did not have anyone to help them. Many did not even know where they were going. At first, they depended on the U.S. government to tell them where to live. Among the main government agencies helping the refugees were the Office of Refugee Resettlement (ORR) and the Immigration and Naturalization Service (INS). The INS (renamed U.S. Citizenship and Immigration Services in 2003) judged whether a refugee could be let into the

A Hmong immigrant girl (*far left*) jumps rope with her new friends in a California schoolyard.

country. The ORR (founded in 1980) had the huge job of helping the refugees once they were admitted. The ORR, however, did not work alone. It was helped by state governments. The state governments, in turn, were helped by a number of voluntary agencies.

Voluntary agencies, or volags, were private groups that often gave direct help to refugees. Some volags were run by religious groups, and some were **secular**. Examples of voluntary agencies that helped Indochinese refugees include the American Council for Nationalities Service and the U.S. Catholic Conference. Volags provided financial support, housing, food, and jobs for refugees. People who wanted to help refugees volunteered to work with these agencies. Some became sponsors. Many sponsors provided food, clothing, and housing for refugees. Some refugees lived with sponsors until they were ready to live on their own. Refugees also got support from other immigrants. Some immigrants joined mutual assistance associations (MAAs). MAA members acted as interpreters for refugees who did not know English and helped them understand American customs. Volags, sponsors, and MAAs also provided basic education about American life. Many refugees had to learn English. They also had to learn about everyday life: how to rent an apartment, how to get medical care, what traffic lights mean, how to use American money, how to use modern appliances. For refugees from rural areas, life in an American city was a new world.

English-as-a-second-language (ESL) programs and job-training programs helped the refugees move toward economic independence. Before they could support themselves, many refugees received money and medical care from the government. In the 1980s, the ORR gave state governments more than $4 billion for refugee aid.

As much as many Southeast Asian Americans want to keep their culture and live among family, many also want to become part of American culture. Irwin Leopando is a Filipino American who first came to the United States in 1995 on a college scholarship. He now teaches English at a college in New York City. He says:

> "Filipino Americans are very family oriented and tend to cluster, especially on the West Coast. And at the same time, Filipino Americans are also very assimilationist. It's a very diverse community. I've met a lot of Filipino Americans who are very proud of their Filipinoness. You know, loud and proud. And I have relatives and friends who think of themselves as more American."

Racism

One of the first challenges immigrants from Southeast Asia faced in the United States was racism. When refugees

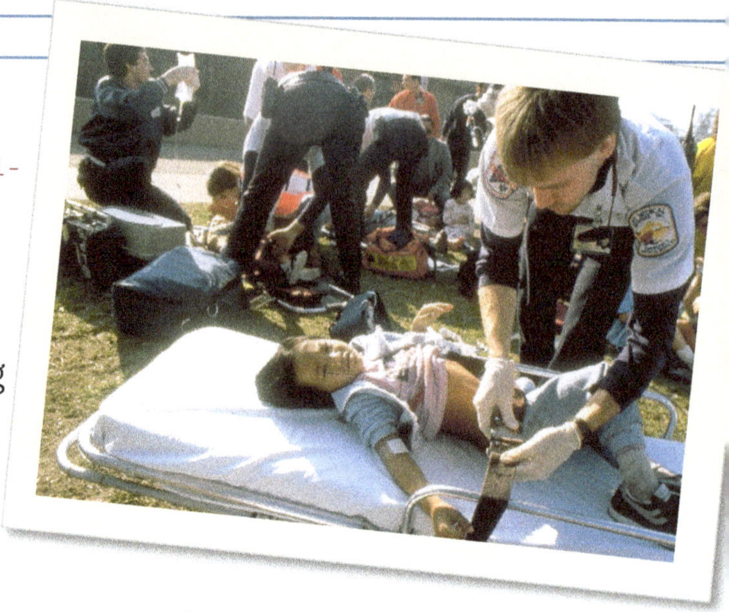

A wounded child is given medical attention after a gunman opened fire on a schoolyard full of Southeast Asian-American children in 1989.

from Vietnam began coming to the United States, many Americans did not welcome their arrival. Some Americans associated the new immigrants with war enemies in spite of the fact that many of the refugees had sided with the United States. At times, Southeast Asian Americans have been threatened or attacked. On January 17, 1989, in Stockton, California, a gunman opened fire on a school playground full of Southeast Asian-American children. The gunman killed five children and wounded twenty-nine other students and a teacher before killing himself. Afterward, a Southeast Asian-American organization in Stockton set the goal of educating others about Southeast Asian Americans and their culture.

New Language, New Jobs

Many Filipino immigrants have benefited from knowing English. Knowing the language of their new country has helped Filipino immigrants succeed in American schools and colleges, the American workforce, and daily life. The majority of the refugees from Vietnam, Laos, and Cambodia did not know English when they came to the United States. The new language they had to learn was very different from their native languages. Some refugees were not **literate** in any language. For older refugees and the illiterate, learning a new language was a major challenge. Many of them never learned English well. Not knowing English limits the types of jobs they can get in the United States. It also means they have to rely heavily on younger family members for everyday activities such as shopping and going to the doctor. The younger generations of Southeast Asian Americans—who came as children or were born in the United States—generally tend not to have trouble with English.

Many of the Filipinos who came to the United States after 1965 were highly educated and skilled professionals who knew English. They were well prepared to make a living in the country. Some educated Filipinos, however, had difficulty taking up their former professions. To practice many professions in the United States, it is necessary to obtain a certificate or license from a professional association or government agency, and often necessary to pass an exam. Doctors have to both pass tests and serve a residency (a period of training in a hospital). Either temporarily or permanently, some Filipino immigrants wound up working at jobs for which they were overqualified. For example, some accountants or pharmacists worked as clerks in hospitals.

Educated refugees from Southeast Asia often ended up working at lower-level jobs than they had previously held. For some, not speaking English well prevented them from continuing their professions or getting good jobs. Many simply wanted to become **self-sufficient** as quickly as possible and were willing to work at whatever jobs they could. They placed

Tommy Xiong, from Laos (in blue shirt), attends a class for English language learners at his Minnesota elementary school.

their work ethic above social status. One former government leader from Vietnam started a lawn-care business in Hawaii.

Different Customs

When immigrants come to a new country, they bring with them practices from their countries of origin. Sometimes these practices, just because they are different, can look strange to the people of their new country. One Filipino immigrant wrote about how an American boy thought it was strange that his wife used an umbrella to protect herself from the bright sun.

Many times, Southeast-Asian immigrants have had a hard time understanding and getting used to American culture. Some Laotians consider ordinary American mannerisms, such as touching and eye contact, to be rude. Although both Americans and Southeast Asians value education, they can have different ideas about it. Many Vietnamese schools, for example, teach students to memorize information and not to question the teacher. Students from Vietnam had to get used to classes in which they were taught to think creatively and ask questions. Sometimes their parents did not understand American education. One Vietnamese teenager remarked: "It took me a long time to understand that I am supposed to talk back to [question] my teacher. My father got very angry at me for doing this, but I will not do well in school if I sit passively and do not ask questions."

At worst, cultural differences with Americans have led to violence. On the Gulf Coast of Texas in 1980, violence erupted between

One Person's Story: Lamthiane Imthirath

Lamthiane Imthirath left Laos with her family in 1975. They went first to Thailand. In 1979, the family moved to Leominster, Massachusetts. In *The Far East Comes Near*, a collection of immigrant biographies edited by Lucy Nguyen-Hong-Nhiem and Joel Martin Halpern, Imthirath described starting school in the United States:

> "During my second week in the United States my sponsors took me to school; I registered. The official said I could start school in a few days. He was pleased to have me as the first Southeast Asian student in school. That particular morning I got up early. I put on my newest clothes, which my sponsors had bought for me. I was full of excitement to meet more people, but deep down inside I felt afraid of something. I spent a little time with other students. I felt uneasy and frustrated when I could not speak English. When other students met me, they would ask what my name was and where I came from. I could not respond, and then they laughed at me. Often I took it the wrong way and got upset with them. I was not an unfriendly person. I wanted so much to express myself and tell them who I was. I think almost every newcomer experiences the communication gap.
>
> "I was very frustrated when I could not speak English so was motivated to learn English faster than others. I was able to communicate with other students within a few months. It was because of my learning ability that I was awarded thirty-five dollars during a Thanksgiving Day rally. . . . The local newspaper interviewed me as the first Southeast Asian student and an outstanding student."

One Person's Story: Van Lu

Van Lu is a college student in New York City. His parents were among the "boat people" who risked their lives to escape from Vietnam. Van, who was born in the United States, talks about some of the challenges of balancing American culture and Vietnamese culture and the importance of having friends who share his experiences:

> "Growing up in a predominantly white, suburban town in the South, I struggled with a way to fit into the all-American mold. Many times, I argued with my parents about the fundamental cultural differences in raising children in Vietnam versus America. I did not understand why they could not grasp the need for slumber parties as a fifth grader or the desire to even date before I turned thirty! However, through this Vietnamese community, I was able to find a common bond through the other first-generation children. Together, at weekly Sunday house parties, we shared our frustrations with growing up as Vietnamese-American children. These moments allowed me to vent to others who would truly understand my sentiments. However, these conversations also brought to light all that we enjoyed about being Vietnamese. We shared our common respect for our parents' abilities to adapt within such a different world and their unrelenting sacrifices to make our lives better. We talked about our love of Sunday parties, unique food, and a sense of belonging with each other. Through this community of young Vietnamese Americans, I learned how to meld the two cultures in which I was brought up, and I found the confidence to embrace all that was different with me."

American and Vietnamese immigrant **shrimpers**. The Vietnamese immigrants, without knowing it, violated customs about fishing territory. They also violated the American custom of keeping boats from bumping one another. In the resulting conflict, some of the American shrimpers burned boats belonging to the Vietnamese shrimpers. Two Vietnamese shrimpers then killed an American shrimper in self-defense. Over time, the Vietnamese shrimpers learned the local customs. The two groups talked and came to respect each other's hard work.

Family Matters

Moving to the United States has had a dramatic effect on the families of Southeast Asian immigrants. In general,

Vietnamese-American shrimpers on the Gulf Coast in Mississippi repair their nets between fishing voyages.

Southeast Asian cultures value the family as a group over any single family member. Traditionally, Southeast Asian children are expected to obey their parents. American culture places greater value on the individual, and American children and teenagers tend to be allowed more freedom. Many older Southeast Asian Americans worry when their children become Americanized, and family conflicts between parents and children can result.

Another major difference between most Southeast Asian cultures and American culture is the role of women. Among traditional Vietnamese, Laotians, Cambodians, and Hmong, men work outside the home to earn money and have the highest authority in the family. Their wives are expected to obey them and focus mainly on domestic life. The need to earn enough money in the United States challenges these roles. Many Indochinese immigrant families need two incomes. Indochinese women who take jobs outside the home often become more independent. Some of them earn more money than their husbands. Many Indochinese men find it hard to cope with the loss of their traditional role and authority. Many of the women, however, like their new roles. Filipino Americans struggle less with this issue. In Filipino culture, husband and wife are more equal than they are in Indochinese cultures.

Young Southeast Asian Americans often feel caught between cultures. A Vietnamese-American teenager spoke about the challenge of having two cultures: "Most of the time I act like an American at school but don't tell my father. At home I follow the Vietnamese customs. It makes it hard, but I am doing okay like that." Many younger Southeast Asian Americans arrived in the United States when they were very young or were born in the United States. These young people grow up with American culture all around. It looks normal to them. Many of their parents and grandparents, however, expect them to pay more attention to traditional ways.

Success Stories

In spite of all the challenges, many Southeast Asian Americans have been very successful in the United States. In 2006, statistics showed that Filipino Americans were better off than the total American population in many ways. On average, they held higher-status jobs, made more money, suffered less from unemployment, and were more likely to have college degrees. Examples of successful Filipino Americans can be found in a wide variety of fields. In the arts, Filipino Americans include professional writers, ballerinas, actors, and singers. In sports, Filipino Americans have distinguished themselves in baseball, football, figure skating, and boxing. Filipino-American doctors include some who are well-known professors of medicine. In

Hawaii, Filipino Americans have been elected to offices in the state government. For example, Filipino American Benjamin J. Cayetano served as governor of Hawaii from 1994 to 2002. Filipino Americans have also held leadership roles in the military. General Antonio Taguba, who was born in the Philippines, became one of the highest-ranking Filipino Americans in the U.S. Army. General Taguba became widely known for issuing a report in 2004 that uncovered abuses by American soldiers at the Abu Ghraib prison in Iraq.

Many Vietnamese Americans are also achieving success in the United States. Although it still falls below that of the overall population, by 2006, Vietnamese-American per capita income had more than doubled since 1990.

As of 2006, Cambodian Americans, Hmong Americans, and Laotian Americans remained behind the overall population in income and education. In spite of the statistics, many members of these groups are moving forward in American society. Many Cambodian Americans who came to the United States with little education and no English skills have become business owners. In Los Angeles, for example, between 80 and 90 percent of the doughnut shops are owned by Cambodian Americans. Cambodian-owned doughnut shops are also common in Texas. In areas with large Hmong communities, many Hmong Americans have started businesses to serve each other. Some of these businesses branch out to serve the larger community. In Milwaukee, a Hmong-owned language interpreting and translation business grew into a bigger business. The company now provides bilingual health-care staff to many other companies.

Filipino Americans celebrate Philippines Independence Day with a parade in New York City.

CHAPTER FIVE

CHANGING THE AMERICAN CULTURE

Southeast Asian-American culture is visible in many ways in the United States, including traditional festivals. Seattle, Washington, holds Festál, a series of cultural festivals that runs throughout the year. In 2008, Festál included three Southeast Asian cultural events. In February, people could go to the Tet Festival, which marks the Vietnamese **Lunar New Year**. In June, one of the Festál events was the Pagdiriwang Philippine Festival, an arts-and-culture event that celebrated Filipino history, art, music, food, and dance. The festival also gave Filipino drill teams, rock bands, and martial artists a chance to perform. In November, Festál attendees could go to the Hmong New Year Celebration.

Filipino-American festivals also include events such as the Festival of Philippine Arts and Culture. Held in San Pedro, California, the 2008 festival featured a variety of Filipino-American singers, musicians, rappers, dancers, and visual artists. A Vietnamese Spring Festival and Parade has been held for many years in San Jose, California. Film festivals have focused on Filipino-American and Vietnamese-American culture. The website HmongFestival.com lists Hmong New Year festivals around the United States. In Los Angeles, there is a Thai New Year Songkran Festival.

Religion

The majority of people in the Philippines are Christian. Likewise, most Filipino Americans are Christians. In some areas, churches serve mainly Filipino Americans and have Filipino-American clergy. For the most part, Filipino-American Christians are Roman Catholic, although some are Protestant. Some Filipino Americans celebrate Christmas with *Simbang Gabi*, a nine-day series of Masses and a feast after the midnight Mass on Christmas Eve.

Most Vietnamese Americans are Buddhists. Buddhism is the traditional religion of Vietnam. Many Vietnamese-American Buddhists have set up temples where they can practice their religion. Their type of Buddhism is Mahayana Buddhism. In some areas, some people were slow to accept Vietnamese Buddhists. To win acceptance, Buddhists in Oklahoma City worked to show people that they embraced American culture. They called their Buddhist temple a "church," sang songs based on Christian hymns, and

This Buddhist temple in Pensacola, Florida, was founded by Vietnamese Americans.

offered free martial arts classes to local children. One Vietnamese-American Buddhist temple that is thriving is located in Pensacola, Florida. An elderly member of the Florida congregation was interviewed in 2008 for an article about the temple in the *Pensacola News Journal*. She said:

> "We left everything, and we lost everything. We had only our spiritual life to take along with us. I grew up in a family of devout Buddhists, so to be able to practice our religion here means a lot. It has helped us survive the hardships we have had to go through."

One study, published in 2000, concluded that about a quarter of all Vietnamese Americans are Christian. Most Vietnamese-American Christians are Roman Catholic. Some Vietnamese Americans combine elements of Buddhism, Catholicism, and other religions into new

Thai food is popular with many Americans. Shown here: shrimp pad thai.

practices. Many Cambodian Americans and Laotian Americans are also Buddhists. Cambodian Americans and Laotian Americans, however, generally practice Theravada Buddhism. Many Hmong Americans practice a traditional **animist** religion, although some are Buddhist or Christian.

Food

Of all the Southeast Asian cuisines, the most popular in the United States is Thai food. Although Thai Americans are a fairly small group, Thai restaurants can be found all over the country. Thai food often uses **curry**. Many Thai dishes are hot and spicy. One of the most popular Thai dishes is pad thai. Pad thai includes rice noodles, egg, tofu, peanuts, and often meat or shrimp. Sriracha is a traditional Thai hot sauce that is also used in Vietnamese cooking. It has become so popular in the United States that it is now made domestically and sold in many supermarkets. Some people use it on fries and hamburgers.

Vietnamese food is also popular around the United States. Well-known Vietnamese dishes include spring rolls and pho. In Vietnamese spring rolls, shrimp and vegetables are wrapped in rice paper. Many Vietnamese restaurants feature large bowls of soup filled with noodles, vegetables, meat, and shrimp. Pho is a beef-and-noodle soup.

Other Southeast Asian cuisines are found mainly near concentrations of Southeast Asian-American people. Filipino restaurants can be found around the country, but most states have very few of them. Although California has by far the most, New Jersey, New York, Florida, and Illinois also have many Filipino restaurants.

Art, Music, Dance, and Other Pastimes

Many Southeast Asian Americans are active in art, music, dance, and literature. They keep alive many traditions. Danongan Kalanduyan is a Filipino-American master of *kulintang* music. Kulintang music is played on gongs. The Apsara Ensemble, a Cambodian-American group, performs Cambodian folk dance.

Hmong Americans are known for making storycloth. Storycloth is based on the traditional Hmong craft of *paj ntaub*. Paj ntaub is the stitching technique that Hmong women use to make traditional costumes. Storycloths are banners in which Hmong women use paj ntaub to illustrate legends and Hmong history. While waiting in refugee camps to be resettled, many Hmong women began making storycloths that showed the Hmong leaving Laos. Hmong-American women sell storycloths at craft fairs and Hmong cultural festivals.

Martial arts from Southeast Asia have become popular in the United States. The Filipino martial arts known as escrima, kali, and arnis emphasize stick fighting and hand

Southeast Asian Americans in Politics

Throughout most of the United States, high-profile Southeast Asian American politicians are rare. One exception is Hawaii. With its long history of Filipino immigration, Hawaii has had many Filipino Americans in its legislature, as well as Filipino American governor Benjamin Cayetano. Filipino Americans have also served in the state governments of such states as West Virginia, Ohio, Maryland, Washington, and Alaska.

In December 2008, Ahn "Joseph" Cao, a Republican from Louisiana, became the first Vietnamese American elected to the U.S. Congress when he won a seat in the House of Representatives. Born in Saigon, Cao came to the United States as a refugee in 1975, when he was eight years old. He eventually settled in New Orleans, where he worked as an immigration lawyer before entering politics. After winning the election in 2008, Cao said, "Never in my life did I think I could be a future congressman. The American dream is well and alive."

Thai American L. Tammy Duckworth was in the national spotlight in 2008 and 2009. Born in Bangkok, Thailand, Duckworth is a member of the Illinois Army National Guard, and she served in the Iraq War. While she was serving in Iraq in 2004, Duckworth's helicopter was hit by enemy fire. She lost both of her legs as a result of the attack. After she recovered, Duckworth began working as an advocate for war veterans. In 2006, she ran for a seat in the U.S. House of Representatives. Duckworth lost the election, but soon after she became director of the Illinois Department of Veterans' Affairs. On Veterans Day 2008, then-President-elect Barack Obama and Duckworth laid a wreath together at a veterans' memorial. In April 2009, she joined the Obama administration as an assistant secretary in the U.S. Department of Veterans Affairs.

Obama himself has connections to Southeast Asia. As a boy, he lived in Indonesia for several years. His half sister, Maya Soetoro-Ng, is Indonesian American.

Ahn "Joseph" Cao celebrates with his family after winning election in 2008 as the first Vietnamese-American member of Congress.

Somali pirates hold 122 Filipinos
(Story below, column 2)

CELEBRATING 37 YEARS 1972-2009

Filipino Reporter

www.filipinoreporter.com
E-mail: filipinoreporter@aol.com
info@filipinoreporter.com

FAIR, FEARLESS, FACTUAL

$1.25 60 PAGES

YEAR XXXVII NO. 19 NATIONAL EDITION — NEW YORK CITY / APRIL 17-23, 2009 — 212.967.5784 • 212.967.7980

IMMIGRATION GETS PRIORITY

Obama wants Congress to act on legalization

WASHINGTON — The Congressional Asian Pacific American Caucus (CAPAC) has lauded President Barack Obama's pronouncement last week that it would begin a major push for immigration reform this year, including a path to citizenship for undocumented workers.

"We all know that the time has come to fix our broken immigration system," the Caucus said in a statement over the weekend. "We need the tax revenues from immigrants already working in our country who want to contribute. We need to make sure families are able to stay together, including families with U.S.-born children. We need fair and practical solutions to make immigration work for our nation, our economy, and our families. We are gratified that President Obama has signaled his intention to begin this important debate in the coming weeks."

Turn to page 8

ALIEN COURTS CLOGGED

WASHINGTON — The nation's immigration courts are now so clogged that nearly 90,000 people accused of being in the United States illegally waited at least two years for a judge to decide whether they must leave, one of the last bottlenecks in a push to more strictly enforce immigration laws.

Their cases — identified by a *USA Today* review of the courts' dockets since 2003 — are emblematic of delays in the little-known court system that lawyers, lawmakers and others say is on the verge of being overwhelmed.

Among them were 14,000 immigrants whose cases took more than five years to decide and a few that took more than a decade.

Turn to page 9

HIJACKED: Wives of Filipino sailors, Doris Deseo, left, and Catherine Boretta, right, show pictures of their husbands Carlo, second from left, and Rodell, second from right, to the Associated Press as they visit the office of a shipping agency in Manila on April 13 to get updates on negotiations to free their hostage husbands in Somalia. (AP photo/Aaron Favila)

Pirates hold 122 Filipino hostages

MANILA — The Philippine Government said on Wednesday that a total of 122 Filipino seafarers are being held by Somali pirates, following the hijacking of a Greek-owned ship with Filipino crew on Tuesday in the Gulf of Aden.

MV Irene E.M. — the latest vessel captured by pirates off Somalian waters — has 22 Filipino seafarers on board, the Philippine Department of Foreign Affairs (DFA) said in a statement.

This is the ninth hijacking in the Gulf of Aden and Indian Ocean since the start of the month.

The DFA said the newly abducted Filipinos are reportedly unharmed and it is continuing to coordinate closely with concerned foreign authorities and the local manning agencies of the hijacked vessels to secure the early and safe release of the Filipino seafarers.

As the number of Filipino hostages keeps swelling in Somalia, the Philippine Government remains clueless on how to provide protection to the thousands of seafarers sailing through the dangerous waters of Africa.

The Philippine Government said that as a policy, it will not negotiate nor pay ransom to the kidnappers.

Turn to page 8

Anchor's wife dies after shot

MANILA — The wife of ABS-CBN news anchor Ted Failon died on Thursday after allegedly committing suicide by shooting herself in the head.

Supt. Franklin Mabanag, the chief of the Crime Investigation and Detection Unit of the Quezon City police, identified

Turn to page 12

Ted Failon undergoes a paraffin test that yielded a negative result.

Manila attorney gets int'l eco award

MANILA — The environmental lawyer who won a landmark case before the Supreme Court last year for the cleanup of Manila Bay has been given an award from an international environmental organization.

OPOSA

Antonio Oposa has been given the 2008 International Environmental Law Award by the Center for International Environmental Law (CIEL), the first Asian to get the award.

The award will be given to Oposa on April 21 in a luncheon in Washington, D.C.

Outstanding contributions

The award recognizes individ-

Turn to page 12

Cebu burial for victim

The body of Dolores Cabunilas-Yigal, the Filipina who was among the 14 people who perished in the Binghamton, N.Y. shooting rampage, will be buried in her native Talisay City, Cebu, Philippines this Sunday (April 19) after being reunited with her family early this week.

Turn to page 9

SOMBER HOMECOMING: Slain Cebuana Dolores Cabunilas-Yigal (l.) with her California-based sister Carmelita C. Swank.

The *Filipino Reporter* newspaper includes content of special interest to Filipino Americans.

techniques. Muay Thai, or Thai boxing, uses both punches and kicks. For some people, Muay Thai is just a spectator sport. Some adults and children, however, take part in Muay Thai classes.

Publications and Organizations

Filipino Americans have been publishing newspapers and magazines since the beginning of the twentieth century. Today, Filipino-American publications include *Filipinas* magazine, which covers Filipino culture, business, and entertainment, and the *Filipino Reporter*. Like many other groups, Filipino Americans take advantage of the Internet. Websites such as TheFilipino.com provide cultural, business, and other links for the Filipino-American community. They also give others the opportunity to learn about Filipino-American culture.

Filipino Americans began forming student groups, cultural groups, and professional organizations in the 1920s and 1930s. Today, there is such a variety of Filipino-American groups that the National Federation of Filipino American Associations organizes and represents them. From religious groups and youth organizations to professional associations and sports groups, Filipino Americans participate in every type of activity. College students of Filipino heritage are active in student cultural organizations. Some colleges and universities have a single organization for all Southeast Asian groups. Columbia University, in New York City, has the Southeast Asian League (SEAL). BeiXian Tang, a past president of SEAL who is from Singapore, says:

> "The Southeast Asian League at Columbia . . . was founded in order to bring awareness of these unique traditions to the student community, as well as to bring Southeast Asian Americans together. Southeast Asia is a rich potpourri of cultures, and we wanted to bring a sense of that to Columbia."

Nguoi-viet.com, the largest Vietnamese-American newspaper, publishes solely online. It was originally written only in the Vietnamese language, but an English version targeted to younger readers was launched in 2004. Organizations such as the Vietnamese American Heritage Foundation promote awareness of the history and culture of Vietnamese Americans. The National Congress of Vietnamese Americans works to help Vietnamese Americans get more involved in politics.

Entertainment and Sports

Some of the most famous Southeast Asian Americans are entertainment and sports figures. Most of these figures have one parent who is Southeast Asian. Famous Filipino Americans include the movie stars Tia Carrere, Lou Diamond Phillips, and Rob Schneider. Figure skating champion Tai Babilonia is a Filipino American. Filipino-American music stars include Broadway star Lea Salonga; rapper apl.de.ap, of the Black Eyed Peas; and guitarist Kirk Hammett, of Metallica. One of the most visible Vietnamese Americans is Betty Nguyen, a CNN newscaster. Danny Graves, a Vietnamese-American baseball player, made the All-Star team in 2000 and 2004. The mother of golf superstar Tiger Woods is a native of Thailand, as is the mother of baseball slugger Johnny Damon. Disney star Brenda Song has a Hmong father and a Thai mother.

Brenda Song starred in the TV movie *Wendy Wu: Homecoming Warrior.*

Today, one of the biggest Southeast Asian-American organizations is SEARAC, or the Southeast Asian Resource Action Center. Founded in 1979, SEARAC works for the benefit of Vietnamese, Cambodian, and Laotian refugees. One of its main goals is to support religious organizations and mutual assistance associations that help resettle refugees. SEARAC also works to keep Southeast Asian Americans informed about many laws and issues that may affect them.

Young Hmong Americans in Minnesota attend graduation-day ceremonies after completing a fourteen-week class to help them adjust to life in the United States.

CHAPTER SIX

LOOKING TO THE FUTURE

Significant numbers of Filipino and Vietnamese immigrants continue to come to the United States. In 2007, 72,596 Filipino immigrants received green cards. "Green card" is the informal name used for the document issued by the U.S. government proving that an immigrant is authorized to be a permanent resident of the United States. Also in 2007, 28,691 Vietnamese received green cards. Filipino and Vietnamese immigrants were the third- and eighth-largest groups to receive green cards. People with green cards can become U.S. citizens after meeting certain requirements. They must be at least eighteen years old, and they must live in the United States for five years in a row. Also, they must show that they have learned English and know the basics of American government and history. In 2007, 38,830 Filipinos became naturalized U.S. citizens, and 27,921 Vietnamese became naturalized. (People born in the United States are automatically U.S. citizens. A naturalized citizen is a person who is born elsewhere and later becomes a U.S. citizen. People who are naturalized have the same full citizenship rights as people born in the United States.)

In some cases, one of the challenges an immigrant to the United States faces is the immigration system itself. In 2008, the *New York Times* reported about the problems faced by a Filipino-American couple, Pedro and Salvacion Servano. The couple's mothers came from the Philippines to the United States in the early 1980s and requested visas for their single children. By the time the visas arrived in 1985, Pedro and Salvacion were married. In the United States, they settled in Pennsylvania. Pedro became a respected doctor, and the couple had four children. In 1991, they got a big surprise when they applied to become citizens as a couple. Authorities saw that they had been married before coming to the United States and concluded that they had lied on their visa applications.

United States-Philippines Dual Citizenship

In 2003, the Philippines passed a law that allows former citizens of the Philippines to again become citizens of that country. Many Filipinos had given up citizenship in the Philippines for American citizenship. Under the new law, these people could become dual citizens, or citizens of both countries. The Philippines also considers the children of any Filipino to be citizens of the country. These children are also dual citizens. Since the new law was passed, thousands of Filipino Americans have become dual citizens. The government of the Philippines wants Filipino Americans to invest in the Philippines and maybe even move there to live. Dual citizenship may pose a challenge for the Filipino-American community if many Filipino Americans choose to take their families, skills, and economic power out of the United States.

A Vietnamese-American girl wearing traditional dress enjoys a Tet (Lunar New Year) celebration in San Jose, California.

They ordered that the Servanos be **deported** (that is, forced to leave the country and return to the Philippines). Seventeen years later, the Servanos were still going through the complicated legal process of opposing their deportation.

Education and Economic Advancement

Filipino Americans will probably continue to advance economically. According to the Census Bureau's 2006 American Community Survey, 36 percent of Filipino Americans of school age or older were in college or graduate school. Many of these people are likely to get high-status jobs in the future. Vietnamese Americans, Cambodian Americans, Laotian Americans, and Hmong Americans may also all be set to advance dramatically in American society.

Vietnamese-American culture greatly values education. Many Vietnamese-American parents push their children to do well in school. The 2006 American Community Survey estimated that almost 34 percent of Vietnamese Americans of school age or older were in college or graduate school. The percentages of Filipino Americans and Vietnamese Americans who are pursuing higher education are far above that of the overall U.S. population. The percentage of Cambodian Americans and Laotian Americans in higher education is about equal to that of the overall U.S. population. Even Hmong Americans—who are economically far behind most Americans—look set to improve their situation. On average, the Hmong-American population is young. The large number of Hmong-Americans enrolled in school in 2006 may well include

A group of Vietnamese-American young men in California relaxes after a game of basketball.

many future college graduates with good career and earnings prospects.

Hmong American Dao Vang now works as a counselor for Southeast Asian-American college students. He describes the importance of education in this way:

> "Education is very, very important for economic advancement. My mother always told me and my brothers that without an education we can't advance in this country. And I believe that, as people of color, education is important to get ahead. I would say that most Southeast Asian–American parents emphasize the importance of education to their kids. But that's not to say that every kid is doing well. Some kids do have problems. If they are caught between cultures and don't know what to do, they can end up in at-risk groups. The ones who aren't comfortable in either culture are most at risk. Students who can live in both their cultures do best."

The Arrest of Vang Pao

In June 2007, Hmong-American Vang Pao was arrested for working to overthrow the government of Laos. Pao was accused of taking part in a plan to buy weapons for Hmong fighters in Laos to use against government buildings. He was arrested by U.S. federal agents in Westminster, California. Pao was one of the Hmong leaders who worked with the U.S. Central Intelligence Agency in Laos during the Vietnam War. He later became a Hmong-American leader. One of his goals was for the Hmong to return to Laos. When he was arrested, Hmong Americans had many different reactions. Some older Hmong Americans were surprised that the U.S. government seemed to have turned against Pao. Many younger Hmong Americans, including those born in the United States, questioned what Pao was doing. Most of them could not relate to Pao's desire to return to Laos. Both young and old Hmong Americans, however, worried that Pao's arrest would stain the image of their people. After his arrest, the school board in Madison, Wisconsin, dropped plans to name an elementary school after Pao. In early 2009, Pao was free on bail awaiting trial.

FACTS ABOUT FILIPINO AMERICANS

Characteristic	Filipino Americans	Percentage for Filipino Americans	Total U.S. Population	Percentage for U.S. Population
Total population	2,328,097		299,398,485	
Male	1,047,644	45%	146,705,258	49%
Female	1,280,453	55%	152,693,227	51%
Median age (years)	38		36	
Under 5 years old	116,405	5%	20,957,894	7%
18 years and over	1,862,478	80%	224,548,864	75%
65 years and over	232,810	10%	35,927,818	12%
Average family size	4		3	
Number of households	664,054		111,617,402	
Owner-occupied housing units	444,916	67%	74,783,659	67%
Renter-occupied housing units	219,138	33%	36,833,743	33%
People age 25 and over with high school diploma or higher	1,512,725	92%	164,729,046	84%
People age 25 and over with bachelor's degree or higher	772,805	47%	52,948,622	27%
Foreign born	1,545,214	66%	37,547,789	13%
Number of people who speak a language other than English at home (population 5 years and older)	1,481,834	67%	55,807,878	20%
Median family income	$78,596		$58,526	
Per capita income	$27,053		$25,267	
Individuals living below the poverty level	116,405	5%	38,921,803	13%

Source: U.S. Bureau of the Census, 2006 American Community Survey estimates

FACTS ABOUT VIETNAMESE AMERICANS

Characteristic	Vietnamese Americans	Percentage for Vietnamese Americans	Total U.S. Population	Percentage for U.S. Population
Total population	1,475,798		299,398,485	
Male	723,141	49%	146,705,258	49%
Female	752,657	51%	152,693,227	51%
Median age (years)	35		36	
Under 5 years old	103,306	7%	20,957,894	7%
18 years and over	1,121,607	76%	224,548,864	75%
65 years and over	118,064	8%	35,927,818	12%
Average family size	4		3	
Number of households	424,026		111,617,402	
Owner-occupied housing units	288,338	68%	74,783,659	67%
Renter-occupied housing units	135,688	32%	36,833,743	33%
People age 25 and over with high school diploma or higher	708,371	72%	164,729,046	84%
People age 25 and over with bachelor's degree or higher	255,801	26%	52,948,622	27%
Foreign born	989,896	67%	37,547,789	13%
Number of people who speak a language other than English at home (population 5 years and older)	1,180,343	86%	55,807,878	20%
Median family income	$55,773		$58,526	
Per capita income	$21,447		$25,267	
Individuals living below the poverty level	206,612	14%	38,921,803	13%

Source: U.S. Bureau of the Census, 2006 American Community Survey estimates

GLOSSARY

alien: A citizen of a country other than the one a person is in.

Amerasian: Referring to Vietnam War–era children, a child of an American father and a Vietnamese mother.

animist: Having to do with the belief in the spirits of nature and nonliving objects.

assimilate: For people who have moved to another country, adopting the customs and behaviors of the people in their new environment.

Communism: A political and economic system in which a powerful government owns land, factories, and other businesses and centrally plans a country's economy. People work for government-owned and government-run enterprises.

Communist: Referring to a country that follows Communism or a person who believes in Communism.

conjoined: Made up of two or more parts that are united.

curry: A powder or paste made of several spices ground together.

deported: Forced to leave a country and return to one's country of origin.

enclave: An area in which a group of people live relatively separately from the surrounding areas.

ethnic: Having to do with the heritage, language, and way of life of the people.

galleon: A type of large, heavy sailing ship used mainly by the Spanish between the fifteenth and eighteenth centuries.

immigrant: A person who travels to another country, usually to settle there.

infrastructure: The system of public works, including transportation, power, water, and sanitation systems, of a country or area.

literate: Able to read and write.

Lunar New Year (Tet): The beginning of the year on a calendar based on the cycles of the Moon.

Malay: Having to do with the culture of the Malay Peninsula and the nearby islands in Southeast Asia.

managerial: Having to do with the job of directing people at work.

median: The number at which a group of numbers divides into two equal parts, half higher and half lower.

nationals: People who are under the protection of a country regardless of citizenship.

peninsula: A piece of land that is surrounded by water on three sides.

per capita: For each person.

permanent resident: When referring to immigration, the status held by an immigrant to the United States who has been approved by the government to live and work permanently there.

refugee: Someone who seeks or takes shelter in a foreign country, especially to avoid war, political persecution, or religious persecution in his or her native country.

secular: Relating to non-religious concerns.

self-sufficient: Able to meet one's own needs.

shrimpers: Fishers who catch shrimp.

visa: A document that indicates a person has permission to enter the United States and to remain either permanently or for a certain period of time.

voluntary agencies: Organizations that help people in emergencies.

TO FIND OUT MORE

Further Reading

Omoto, Susan. *Hmong Milestones in America: Citizens in a New World.* Evanston, IL: John Gordon Burke Publisher, 2002.

Snyder, Gail. *Filipino Americans*. Philadelphia: Mason Crest, 2009.

Sonneborn, Liz. *Vietnamese Americans*. New York: Chelsea House, 2006.

Sterngass, Jon. *Filipino Americans*. New York: Chelsea House, 2007.

Streed, Sarah. *Leaving the House of Ghosts: Cambodian Refugees in the American Midwest*. Jefferson, NC: McFarland & Company, 2002.

Websites

http://www.asian-nation.org
Asian-Nation contains information and links for and about the Asian-American community.

http://www.filipinoamericanlibrary.org
The website of the Filipino American Library includes an interactive time line of Filipino-American history.

http://www.u.arizona.edu/~falk/pdf/se_womenseyes.pdf
A virtual slideshow that includes information about the cultural lives and professional achievements of a variety of Southeast Asian-American women.

BIBLIOGRAPHY

The author found these sources especially helpful when researching this volume:

Bautista, Veltisezar. *The Filipino Americans from 1763 to the Present: Their History, Culture, and Traditions*. Warren, MI: Bookhaus Publishers, 2002.

Faderman, Lillian, with Ghia Xiong. *I Begin My Life All Over: The Hmong and the American Immigrant Experience*. Boston: Beacon Press, 1998.

Hein, Jeremy. *From Vietnam, Laos, and Cambodia: A Refugee Experience in the United States*. Woodbridge, CT: Twayne Publishers, 1995.

Nguyen-Hong-Nhiem, Lucy, and Joel Martin Halpern. *The Far East Comes Near: Autobiographical Accounts of Southeast Asian Students in America*. Amherst: University of Massachusetts Press, 1989.

Rutledge, Paul James. *The Vietnamese Experience in America*. Bloomington: Indiana University Press, 1992.

The author conducted personal interviews with the following people quoted in this book, and the author and publisher wish to thank them for their cooperation:

Irwin Leopando, Van Lu, BeiXian Tang, Dao Vang

Notes:

Chapter 3:

Page 35: "[A]ll of these people were trying to get on the plane at the airport. . ." Takaki, Ronald. *Strangers from a Different Shore: A History of Asian Americans*. New York: Penguin Books, 1989.

Page 37: "Around 9:00 P.M. on June 4, 1979, . . . " Nguyen-Hong-Nhiem, Lucy, and Joel Martin Halpern. *The Far East Comes Near: Autobiographical Accounts of Southeast Asian Students in America*. Amherst: University of Massachusetts Press, 1989.

Chapter 4:

Page 51: "It took me a long time to understand . . . " Rutledge, Paul James. *The Vietnamese Experience in America*. Bloomington: Indiana University Press, 1992.

Page 51: "During my second week in the United States . . . " Nguyen-Hong-Nhiem, Lucy, and Joel Martin Halpern. *The Far East Comes Near: Autobiographical Accounts of Southeast Asian Students in America*. Amherst: University of Massachusetts Press, 1989.

Page 54: "Most of the time I act like an American at school . . . " Rutledge, Paul James. *The Vietnamese Experience in America*. Bloomington: Indiana University Press, 1992.

All websites were accessible as of March 29, 2009.

INDEX

Page numbers in **boldface** are illustrations, tables, and charts.

Amerasians, 40
arts and entertainment, 54, 57–58, 61–63, 65, **65**
assimilation, 11, 47, 48–50, 52–54

Babilonia, Tai, 65
"boat people," **38**, 39
Buddhism, 58–60, **59**
Bunker, Chang and Eng, 26, **26**
Burmese, 27, 42–43, **43**
  see also Myanmar
business ownership, 50, 55

California, **6**, 7, **8**, 9, **12**, 15, 22, 25, 27, **28**, **41**, **44**, **46**, 48, **48**, 58, 61, **69**, **70**
Cambodia, 9, 10, **10**, 32, 33–35, **34**
Cambodians, 9, **11**, 13, 27, 42, 53, 55, 60
Cao, Ahn "Joseph," 62, **62**
Cayetano, Benjamin J., 55, 62
children, 40, **46**, 48, **48**, 50–51, **50**, 53, 54
citizenship, **5**, 25, 67–69
Communism, 10, 31, 32, 33, 37
crime and violence, 25, 48, **48**, 51–52
cultural differences, 50–54

discrimination and prejudice, 25, 40, 47–48
Dith Pran, 34, **34**

education, 21, 22, **50**, 70, 71
  cultural differences, 50–51
ethnic communities, 5, **6**, 14, **14**, 15

family, 30, **43**, 47, 52–54
festivals and celebrations, **56**, 57–58, **69**
Filipinos, 9, 11, **11**, **12**, 13, 15, **16**, 30, **30**, 31, 47, 58, **72**
  arts and entertainment, 61, 65
  careers, **28**, 29, 48, 49, 54–55, 62
  citizenship issues, 67–69
  festivals and celebrations, **56**, 57–58
  history of immigration, 17–19, 22–25
  publications and organizations, 63, **63**, 64
  servicemen, 23, **24**
food, 14, 60–61, **60**
France, 31–32

government and politics, 20, 55, 62, **62**

Hawaii, **12**, 22, 23, 55, 62
Hmong, 9, 10, 11, **11**, **44**, **46**, 55, 60, **66**, 70–71
  civil war, participation in, 32, 33
  communities, 14, **14**
  festivals and celebrations, 57, 58
  poverty, reasons for, 13, 14, 15
  refugees, coming of, **41**, 42
  storycloths, 61
Ho Chi Minh, 32

immigration
  causes of, 27, 30, 37, 39, 42
  impact of, 4, 15, 23, 60
  laws on, 29, 30, 35, 39, 40
Immigration and Nationality Act of 1965, 29, 30, 39

Immigration and Naturalization Service (INS), 45, 46
Indochina Migration and Refugee Assistance Act of 1975, 35
Indochina, 9, 10, **10**
Indonesia, 10, **10**

Japan, 22, 23, 31
jobs and careers, 11, 13, 23, **28**, 49

Khmer Rouge, 33, 34, 35, 42
Killing Fields, The (movie), 34

language skills, 11, 13, 47, 48–49
Laos, 9, 10, **10**, 32, 33, 71
Laotians, 9, 11, **11**, 13, 15, 27, 32, 41–42, **50**, 53, 55, 60
Little Saigon, **6**, 7, 15
Los Angeles, California, 15, 55, 58

Manilamen, **16**, 17–18
marriage, 18, 23, 25, 27
martial arts, 61, 63
media, 22, 63, 64
medical professionals, **28**, 29, 49
Minnesota, 9, 14, **14**, **50**, **66**
Montagnards, 40, 41
movies, 34, 65, **65**
mutual assistance associations (MAAs), 46
Myanmar (Burma), 10, **10**, 42

Ngor, Haing S., 34, **34**

Office of Refugee Resettlement (ORR), 45–46, 47
Orderly Departure Program, 39
organizations, 46, 64, 65

Pao, Vang, 71
parents, 40, 51, 53, 54
pensionados, **21**, 21–22
personal histories, 37, 40, 51, 52
Philippines, 9, 10, **10**, 17, 19, 23, 24, 58, 68
  colony, as, 18, **19**, 20
Pol Pot, 33
population distribution, **8**, 9, **12**
poverty, 13, 39
prejudice. *See* discrimination and prejudice

racism, 47–48, **48**
Refugee Act of 1980, 39
refugees, 13, 33, 35–37, **38**, 39–43
religion, 58–60

Saigon, Vietnam, 33, 35, **36**
shrimpers, 52, **53**
social services, 37, 46, 47
Song, Brenda, 65, **65**
Soviet Union, 31
Spain, 17, 18–19
Spanish-American War, 18–19
sports, 54, 65
Stockton, California, 48, **48**

Taguba, Antonio, 55
Thai, 10, **11**, 15, 42, 60, **60**, 63
Thailand, 10, **10**, 39, 42

U.S. Census Bureau, 9, 11, 69
U.S. Navy, 18–19, 23

Vietnam, 9, 10, **10**, 31–32, 36, 58
  economic conditions, 37, 39
Vietnamese, **8**, 9, 13, 27, 55, 64, **73**
  Amerasian children, 40
  communities, **6**, 7, 15
  cultural differences, 51, 52
  education, role of, 70
  festivals, 57, **69**
  food, 60–61
  religion, 58–59
  waves of refugees, 35–37, **36**, **38**, 39
Vietnam War, 10, 13, 32–33, 41
voluntary agencies, 37, 46

wages and income, 13, 55
Westminster, California, **6**, 7, 15, 71
Wisconsin, 9, 14, 55
women, 53, 61
World War II, 23, **24**

yo-yo, 23

About the Series Consultant

Judith Ann Warner is a Professor of Sociology and Criminal Justice at Texas A&M International University (TAMIU), located in Laredo, Texas, near the U.S.-Mexico border. She has specialized in the study of race and ethnic relations, focusing on new immigrants to the United States and their social incorporation into American society. Professor Warner is the editor of and contributed a number of essays to *Battleground Immigration* (2009), a collection of essays on immigration and related national security issues. Recognition of her work includes the 2007 Distance Educator of the Year Award and the 1991 Scholar of the Year Award at TAMIU.

About the Author

New York–based writer and editor Alan Wachtel has worked on educational books since 2001. He likes to tell people he leads a complicated double life that sometimes calls for use of his trusty grappling hook. This is his first book for Marshall Cavendish Benchmark.